Translated from Dutch by Polly Lawson
First published in English in 1997 by Floris Books, 15 Harrison Gardens, Edinburgh.
© 1997 Christofoor Publishers, Zeist. English version © Floris Books 1997
British Library CIP Data available ISBN 0-86315-255-4 Printed in Belgium

Rebecca Rabbit
Plays Hide-and-Seek

A story by Evelien van Dort
Illustrated by Truus van der Haar

Floris Books

Rebecca Rabbit loved playing hide-and-seek with her brothers and sisters. The red squirrel, the mouse, and the hedgehog sometimes joined in, but Rebecca always knew the best hiding places.

"Rebecca, where are you?" her big brother called.

He looked everywhere but couldn't see her. Was that a blade of grass moving? Quickly he jumped into the long grass. There was Rebecca hiding with her ears pressed flat.

"Found you!" called her brother.

Soon it was Rebecca's turn to hide again. This time the squirrel climbed high up among the leaves of an oak tree to look for her. He peeped through the branches. Where was she hiding?

The squirrel couldn't see Rebecca anywhere. But she could see him.

The squirrel stayed quite still and listened carefully. Where was that rustling noise? Was it the wind in the branches? — or was it perhaps Rebecca ...?

Quickly the squirrel scampered down the tree. Among the bushes he saw a white bushy tail. There was Rebecca Rabbit nibbling the grass! The squirrel pulled her tail and called "Found you!"

Soon it was dark in the woods and all the animals went to sleep.

The next morning the animals played hide-and-seek again.
Rebecca went to hide first. The little grey mouse had to find her.

The mouse looked under the trees, among the leaves and
moss, and over by the sandy hill. Rebecca was nowhere to be
found.

"Peep, peep, who can help me?" the little mouse squeaked. All the rabbits came running from the wood, together with the squirrel and the hedgehog.

"I can't find Rebecca anywhere," the mouse said sadly.

"Let's all have a look," said the hedgehog, giving her a hug.

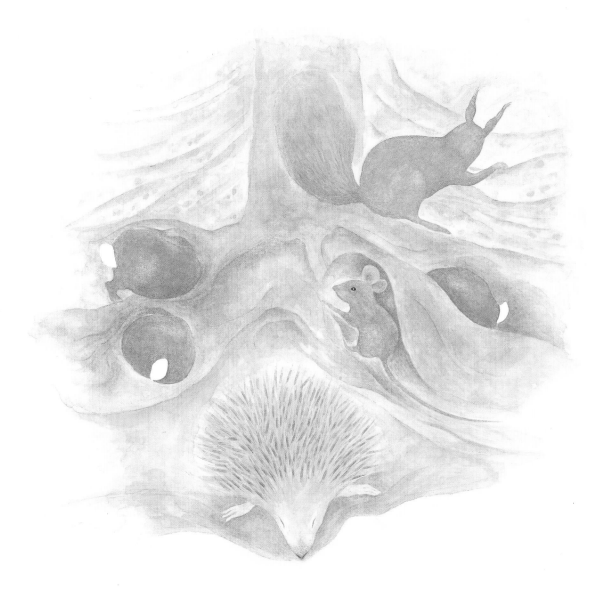

The rabbits looked in the burrows, and the squirrel looked
among the low branches. The hedgehog sniffed among the leaves
and the mouse looked between the roots of the trees. But there
was no sign of Rebecca Rabbit.

By the afternoon the animals were tired of looking. They all called out together, "Rebecca, where are you?"

What a noise they all made! But when they listened for an answer, there was only silence.

"Let's go to see the wise owl," they decided, and off they went. The owl lived in a tree-trunk at the edge of the wood and slept all day. Who was going to wake her up?

"Not me," said the mouse.

"I'll go," said the squirrel. He climbed the tree and disappeared into the hole in the tree.

Sleepily the wise owl came out of the hole and blinked her eyes.

"So Rebecca Rabbit has disappeared," she said. She thought very deeply.

"What is Rebecca's favourite food?" she asked at last. "Fresh grass or roots?"

"Brambles," said Rebecca's brother. "Rebecca loves sweet juicy brambles."

"Then go up to the moorland where the brambles grow," said the owl.

"That's a good idea. Thank you!" they all cried, and ran off as fast as they could.

Puffing and panting they came to the brambles. And now they heard a soft cry from the middle of the bushes. "Help me!"

There was Rebecca Rabbit sadly huddled. "I was hiding in the brambles when I saw a big, juicy berry. But then I got stuck in the prickles and I can't get out," she wailed.

"Poor Rebecca! How can we help" the animals asked.

"I can slip between the thorns and gnaw through the brambles
with my sharp teeth," said the mouse.

No sooner said than done. And soon Rebecca Rabbit came
happily out of the brambles with the mouse.

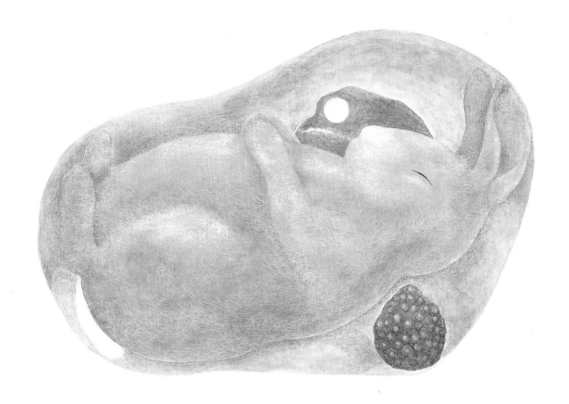

After her adventure, Rebecca was glad to be home again. All the animals were tired at the end of an exciting day. They curled up in their burrows and holes as the day ended, and soon went to sleep. Except for the wise owl, who was starting to wake up.